"A treat to read about Oscar's escapades in London. Loved when he met the Queen! Fabulous illustrations, too."
Abi Elphinstone, author of Rumblestar

"In her latest book for children, I'm sure Molly Arbuthnott's fans will be delighted to catch up with the eventful lives of Oscar and Mercy – this time moving in royal circles – and again enchantingly illustrated by Agnes Treherne.
Mary Sheepshanks, author

"Oscar is a very special and brave cat! Not many cats have the courage and discipline to lead the Queen's Guard and meet the Queen. A great story that captures the long and proud military tradition that is the Queen's Guard.
I wonder where Oscar will go next…?
Major Thomas Mortensen Scots Guards,
One of the Captains of the Queen's Guard

"It is a really lovely story. I am sure all young children will enjoy it enormously!"
Richard Townend, Headmaster of Hill House

OSCAR THE LONDON CAT

ISBN: 978-1-912535-78-1

Edit & layout Shaun Russell

Published by
Jelly Bean Books
Mackintosh House
136 Newport Road, Cardiff, CF24 1DJ
www.candyjarbooks.co.uk

Printed and bound in the UK by
Severn, Bristol Road, Gloucester, GL2 5EU

OSCAR the LONDON CAT

Molly Arbuthnott

illustrated by Agnes Treherne

Oscar and Mercy were quite happy with their ferry life. They couldn't imagine being anywhere else. They had their friends, routine, and hoped that nothing would ever change.

The ferry was expecting a very important visitor. A hot and sweaty Colin the captain was racing around the ferry checking everything was spick and span.

Then all they had to do was wait…

    and wait…
        and wait.
  Finally, a man dressed in the
smartest uniform Oscar had
ever seen came striding
onto the ferry.

"Hello, Captain James," Colin the captain gushed, racing over with his arm out-stretched.

"Good evening, sir!" Captain James said.

"Come and make yourself at home," Colin the captain said. "Would you like a stiff whiskey?" he asked as he led Captain James into his cabin.

The cats were very confused. Why were there now two captains on the ferry? Did James run a ferry too? Where was it?

Pondering such questions, they started walking to their beds, but stopped when they spotted a black furry hat.

"That looks comfy," Oscar remarked. So, they both curled up inside it and went to sleep.

They awoke to the sounds of cars and sirens.
"Where are we?" Mercy cried.

The cats poked their heads out from inside the hat and didn't recognise their surroundings at all. All they saw were lots of houses and lots of people.

What pickle have we got ourselves into this time? thought Oscar.

Eventually, the cats gingerly climbed out. There were hundreds of people all dressed in smart red uniforms marching around.

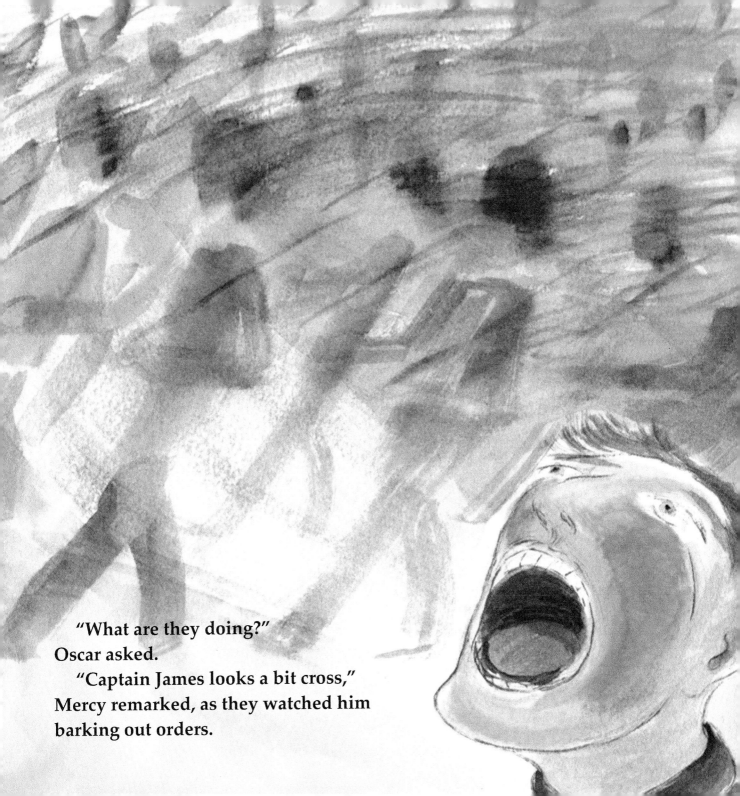

"What are they doing?"
Oscar asked.

"Captain James looks a bit cross," Mercy remarked, as they watched him barking out orders.

"What are you two doing here?" Captain James asked, having spied the cats. "OK, there isn't time," he snapped. "Sit up here and keep out of the way. We are getting ready for changing of the guard," he explained hurriedly as he raced off.

The two cats sat and watched as men marched past. Left, right, left, right, left... out into the sunlight.

"Come on, Corporal Cruachan," Captain James said to a highland Pony. He pulled hard on the reigns and wafted carrots in front of Cruachan's nose, but the pony refused to move.

He refused and refused,
until he snorted and
stomped all over
Captain James' smart
black boots.

"What do we do now,
sir?" the troops
panicked.

Captain James suddenly remembered the cats! He raced over to Oscar and Mercy. "Could you lead the troops as their mascot?" he asked. Oscar thought about this and, linking his paw with Mercy's, calmly replied, "We will only go together."

A nd so it came to pass, that one hot June day the Queen's guard were led up to Buckingham Palace by two very proud cats walking perfectly in time as if they had been born to the job.

They were given the most humungous applause and had to come back to give a second bow to the thrilled crowds.

As they started walking towards the peace and quiet of Wellington Barracks, Captain James raced after them shouting, "Stop! Please follow me. There is someone who would like to meet you."

The cats followed Captain James back to Buckingham Palace, and into a very smart room.

There, sitting behind a table laden with tea things, was the Queen.

"I wanted to personally thank the heroes of the day," she said, presenting both Oscar and Mercy with a medal.

"Thank you, Your Majesty," they said.

They all enjoyed a very jolly tea together.

The next day the Queen organised a private helicopter to take Oscar and Mercy back to their ferry. Colin the captain couldn't believe his eyes as the helicopter landed on his ferry and the two cats hopped out.

"What *have* you two been up to now?" Colin the captain asked.

"Just a usual day for us…" Oscar and Mercy replied as they skipped off.

For Uncle James and those playing
their part in our armed forces.

OSCAR the HEBRIDEAN CAT

Also available Oscar the Hebridean Cat

IN SUPPORT OF
SCOTTY'S LITTLE SOLDIERS

The charity for children of the fallen

CHARITY NO 1136854